Leigh Robinson

Joseph E. Johnston

Leigh Robinson

Joseph E. Johnston

ISBN/EAN: 9783337307653

Printed in Europe, USA, Canada, Australia, Japan

Cover: Foto ©Raphael Reischuk / pixelio.de

More available books at **www.hansebooks.com**

JOSEPH E. JOHNSTON.

AN ADDRESS

DELIVERED BEFORE

THE ASSOCIATION OF EX-CONFEDERATE SOLDIERS AND
SAILORS OF WASHINGTON, D. C.,

—BY—

LEIGH ROBINSON,

MAY 12, 1891,

AT THE MEMORIAL SERVICE HELD IN

MT. VERNON M. E. CHURCH, SOUTH,

AND THE PROCEEDINGS OF THE OCCASION.

Published by the Association.

WASHINGTON, D. C.:
R. O. POLKINHORN, PRINTER,
1891.

INTRODUCTORY.

The Association of ex-Confederate soldiers and sailors of Washington, D. C., met in Mount Vernon Place M. E. Church on May 12th, 1891, at 8 p. m. A large number of the friends of the association and citizens of Washington and Alexandria were present. GEN. EPPA HUNTON presided. The proceedings were opened with prayer by REV. J. F. WIGHTMAN, D. D.

PRAYER.

"O Lord, thou wast our father's God, and thou art our God. We invoke thy presence and thy benediction. Thou art the righteous disposer of human affairs, and we meekly bow to thy sovereign will. Thy finger has marked the boundary of all lands, and we receive our land from Thee; a land flowing with milk and honey. We give Thee humble thanks for the endurement of our civil and religious liberties, for our laws, our homes, our institutions of benevolence, our schools of learning, and for all the benefits of the means of grace. We give thanks to Thee for the gift of good and great men who have directed the affairs of our people, alike in times of peace and amid the troubles of war. We are unworthy, O Lord, of these manifold blessings, and we beseech Thee pardon the transgressions of our people for the sake of thy Son. Thou hast most graciously promised to honor the people that honor Thee; be pleased in thy tender mercy to look upon thy servant, the President of these United States, and upon all

who are empowered to make our laws and to uphold
the majesty of government, that we may live a quiet
and peaceable life in all godliness. We beseach
Thee grant to our people remunerative labor, screen
them from the disasters of life, protect their morals,
quiet all civil dissensions, suppress all evils, bless
our children, and grant to our homes peace and
prosperity, that this great commonwealth may glorify
that name in the virtues and valor of good citizens.
Would it please Thee to unite all sections of this
country in brotherly concord, that Ephraim may no
longer envy Judah, nor Judah vex Ephraim. Hasten
the day when from the North to the South, and from
the East to the West, our mountains shall nod in
homage to Thee, and our cities shall clasp their
hands in praising the name of the Lord. Overrule
for good, we meekly beseach Thee, all national
trouble, the sickness of our people, and the calami-
ties of war, that the discipline of thy providence
may make us wiser and better. Grant, we pray
Thee, that the heroic deeds and noble virtues of our
great soldiers may only inspire us to cherish the
liberty and defend the land that Thou hast given
us. We render thanks to Thee for the honored name
of the Christian soldier whose worth we commemo-
rate on this memorial evening. Be Thou the Father
of his family, and the Guardian of all his comrades
in arms. Hasten the day, O Lord, when all officers
in the field, and all our armies, both upon the land
and the sea, shall fight the good fight of faith, and
make a holy surrender to the great Captain of our
salvation. Would it please Thee to inspire Thy
servant who shall speak to us on this memorial occasion, and so touch his lips with the generous coal
of Thy grace, that he may set forth for Thy glory
those virtues of the fallen hero, that may incite in us
true patriotism and fidelity to the God of our fathers.
Thou hast said, 'Blessed is the nation whose God is
the Lord, and the people whom he hath chosen for
his own inheritance.' The Lord our God be with
us as he was with our fathers. Let him not leave

us nor forsake us. Grant this, we beseech Thee,
through the name and mediation of our Lord, Jesus
Christ. Amen."

———

The Chant, "Abide with Me," was then rendered
by a quartet of the Church Choir.

———

The following verses of a Union Soldier, were, by
request, read by Father W. R. COWARDIN, of St.
Aloysius Chuch, who prefaced the reading with these
words of explanation :

Mr. CHAIRMAN, Ladies and Gentlemen, Confederate
Veterans ; coming, as they do, from one who fought
in the Union Army against him, whose memory we
are here to honor, the verses, I am about to read,
seem to be an answer to the prayer, just offered, for
peace and union in this dear land. They are written by Mr. C. E. MORTON, a soldier of the Mexican
War, who served there under General JOHNSTON, by
whom he was promoted, on the field of battle at
Chapultepec, for gallantry. He sends the verses with
the request that they be read here to-night, as a
tribute to the memory of one he held in high esteem.
The sentiment of the verses is beautiful, and in
paying just tribute to three illustrious heroes of
the Confederacy, JOHNSTON, Jackson and Lee—he
rises above all sectional hatred and shows a magnanimity of soul becoming a great man.

JOSEPH E. JOHNSTON.

We mourn not gallant JOHNSTON dead,
For lives like his well spent, well sped,
  Are not fit themes for grief ;
He leaves a record proud and high :
As he did heroes live and die,
  Be life prolonged, or brief.

His star arose that far-off day,
When, bleeding, almost dead, he lay
  Where Cerro Gordo frowns,
Where his reconnaisance preserved
So many lives, that it deserved
  The mural crown of crowns.

And he was foremost in the fray
At Casa Mata's Mills—"del Rey "--
  Where we fought one to four,
Where higher than at Waterloo,
For ninety minutes carnage flew,
  Red-robed in Aztec gore.

At Montezuma's ancient keep--
Chapultapec--his accents deep
  Cheered the chec'k stormers on ;
Still leading, animating all,
Until we forced the city wall,
  And Mexico was won.

Though I lament the choice he made
When yielding his still stainless blade
  In anti Union strife,
I know he deemed it duty done,
Dire duty, as Virginia's son
  Owed her both fame and life.

Earth smiling at the praise or blame
Of South or North, asserts her claim.
  To JOHNSTON, Jackson, Lee ;
Fame shrines them in her place of pride,
And justly;--no such soldiers died
  At thee, Thermopylæ !

GENERAL HUNTON then said :

Gentlemen of the Association of ex-Confederate Soldiers and Sailors of Washington City.

LADIES AND GENTLEMEN: It is a great privilege to meet together as Confederates in this association, the object of which is to help the needy, to cheer the disheartened, to rejoice with those who rejoice, and weep with those who weep, and especially to eulogize the virtues of the good and great who go before us.

I have greatly rejoiced at the formation of this society, and hope it will last as long as Washington city holds any survivors of the dear lost cause.

We cannot meet to celebrate the success of that cause, but we can and do meet to recount the hardships we endured, the sacrifices we made, the victories we won, the defeats we suffered while battling for that cause, which we believed to be as just and sacred as ever animated a patriotic people.

I feel greatly honored in presiding over your deliberations on any occasion—but especially honored to preside over a meeting called to honor the memory of one of the greatest and best of our leaders—General JOSEPH E. JOHNSTON.

He was the last but one of the six Confederate Generals who led our armies to victory, or in defeat inspired them to greater deeds of valor.

I enjoyed the privilege of knowing General JOHNSTON from an early period of the war; was his colleague in the Congress of the United States, and from the time he entered Congress till his death, I was honored with his confidence, respect and friendship.

Whether at the head of a victorious or vanquished army, he was always the brave, skilful and trusted leader.

In the councils of this nation he was the watchful guardian of his peoples' interest.

In private life he was the patriotic and honored

8

citizen, and the warm and sympathetic friend. In the domestic circle he was the devoted and affectionate husband and tender relative. If I had to name the virtue which shone most conspicuously in his bright character, I would say it was the love of his State—his own beloved Virginia. For her and in obedience to her call he sacrificed a high position and a brilliant future in the Federal army to do battle in her defence. To the last moment of his life he looked to her as the child to a beloved mother, and at any time was willing to sacrifice all—even life itself—for her. It is meet and proper that we his followers and survivors, should cherish and honor his memory and emulate his virtues.

I congratulate the Association on the selection of the the orator who will in glowing and eloquent language. tell of the virtues and fame of our departed leader and friend. The Confederacy had no braver, truer or better soldier than our orator for this evening. His career in the army was not so brilliant as that of General JOHNSTON, but his life was as pure, his patriotism was as great, and his courage was as high and noble as of any soldier who followed the "Stars and Bars" through four years of bloody war.

I introduce my friend Mr. LEIGH ROBINSON, of Washington City, who will now address you :

ADDRESS.

"Death makes the brave my friends," was the great word of the great Crusader; and though the outward empire of the chivalry he led has crumbled to dust, and "their swords are rust," the intrinsic nobleness thereof survives the first crusade and the last. Wherever nobleness has a house, there shall this gospel also be preached. Nor can it be said to be strictly bounded by the noble. The emulation of brave lives, and the preservation of their images, is the wise instinct of mankind. The path to immortality is fortitude. In every noble arena this is the crucial test. The corner-stone of every fortress of man's power and man's honor is man's fortitude. Our inmost shrines are altars to this tutelary god. Deep in the heart is the sense of that ineradicable royalty which makes the crown of thorns more than the crown of gold—martyr more than victor. It is the true-fixed, the constant quality, that hath no fellow in the firmament. Constancy is the pole on which the heavens turn.

As one who wore this armor against fate, and walked erect beneath it till forescore had been passed: as one who in all relations evinced the enduring fibre which sets the seal on every excellence—JOSEPH E. JOHNSTON is our theme. We are to consider the example of a life which by birth was martial. To the son of one Lee's Legion, nourished by the breath of heroes, in the heroic prime, a soldier's life seemed the natural office of a soldier's son. A cadetship at West Point was the signal that the parade ground of his life was chosen, the tuition of his destiny begun, the Olympian battle joined. "Better," sings an ancient bard, "better is the grave than the life of him who sighs when the horns summon him to the squares of battle." So, sighed not the young second lieutenant, who graduating with honor in 1829, first won his spurs in the Florida war.

The war itself must be acknowledged to be a part of that sad chapter, which registers the uncontained avidity of a victor race. When, in July, 1821, Spain ceded the Floridas to the United States, the Indians were roaming unmolested over the Peninsula, and were the recognized possessors of broad and fertile acres in the heart of the country. The white man's remedy for this is the tangle of treaties, from whose net-work the Indian emerges a desolating savage. It is ever a perilous moment, when weakness is the guard of fertility and rapacity is strong. But it is when, in the sequel, devastation and havoc have been loosed, and tottering age, and infantile weakness, and woman's sorrow are alike devoured by infuriated murder, that the army appears upon the scene. Whatever was the primary right or wrong, our young second lieutenant was in the field, not for outrage, but to quell it. He was there to act a soldier's part in the school of a soldier's strife and duty. Right worthily he did it. For it fell to him to extricate from jeopardy the command in which he was himself but a subordinate ; a jeopardy so great that it left him with the marks of five bullets on his person and clothing. On the anvil of an *indomitable will he was already beating into polished brightness the fearless mettle of his soul. Henceforth, his "baptism of fire" stands sponsor for him. His knighthood has been laid upon his shoulder.

It is the track of the accomplished knight which we follow in the war with Mexico—that ardent nurse of heroes—where our Second Lieutenant has grown to be Captain of Engineers on the staff of Winfield Scott. When Vera Cruz yielded to bombardment, Captains Robert E. Lee and JOSEPH E. JOHNSTON, of the general's staff, were appointed to arrange the terms of its surrender. Worthier ambassadors of victory could not have been chosen..

The army then moved along the great national road, made by the old Spaniards, to the ancient capital of Mexico. On April 12th, 1847, cannon shots from Cerro Gordo checked the cavalry advance, and made it certain Santa Anna would give battle there. At the head of a pass, winding its ascending way through a narrow defile of mountains, the enemy had fortified himself by a series of breastworks, armed with cannon, which commanded the road and each other. It was easy to see that, on the left, the position could not be taken. Skillful reconnoissances, in which JOHNSTON bore a conspicuous part, decided the plan of battle, which was an attack upon the right. At the beginning of the assault, JOHNSTON was ordered to make one more reconnoissance. The rattle of musketry had been heard but a few minutes, when he fell, severely wounded, at the head of his daring movement. Of such is the king-

dom of victory! There is the dangerous pass: there
the difficult height: there the hero's place: there he
falls! An army rushes over him to triumph. So
the steep cone was carried—"the lofty and difficult height of Cerro Gordo,"—as the commanding
general called it.

A soldier's wounds are the rounds in his ladder.
His letter of credit is written in his blood. His noble traffic is the safety of others in return for blows
to himself. Johnston's wounds pointed to him as
the fit man to be Lieutenant Colonel of the line regiment of Voltiguers. At their head he led the assault upon Chapultepec, and at their head he was
again shot down. But his wounds could not impede
him from entering the City of Mexico, as Command-
ant of the regiment he had so gallantly led.

After the war, he was, for a time acting Inspector-
General. Still later, he was made Lieutenant-Colo-
nel of Cavalry. Finally, he was appointed Quarter-
master, with the rank of Brigadier,—the highest
prize which was then accessible.

Such was the prologue to the more stupendous
drama upon which the curtain was now to rise. On
one side of that curtain hung every ambitious hope,
the fruition whereof might now be counted sure;
on the other the strain of an unequal and untried
power against the odds of number and organized resource. To choose the latter was to plunge into an
angry flood which might prove the dark abyss. It
was the leap from sure eminence into the storm and
roar of the elements. To Johnston there was no
alternative. His choice was the hero's choice,—where
the sacrifice was all that was certain. The forlorn

hope had ever been his hope. He forsook the assured eminence for the earthquake of revolution ; to stand or fall with the soil it rocked. It was the peril of everything, only to be justified, if principle was at stake. JOHNSTON's justification can be given in no words better than his own. I believed, he says, "that apart from any right of secession, the revolution begun was justified by the maxims so often repeated by Americans, that free government is founded on the consent of the governed, and that every community strong enough to establish and maintain its independence has a right to assert it. Having been educated in such opinions, I naturally determined to return to the State of which I was a native, join the people, among whom I was born, and live with my kindred, and, if necessary, fight in their defense."

It was but little more than a decade since JOHN-STON had freely shed his blood in a war, which grew out of our very willing vindication of the right of Texas to secede from Mexico, and accede to the Union. The United States, somewhat loudly, proclaimed to the world that this was right. A President had been elected for triumphing in that cause. It was natural for JOHNSTON to believe, that a right, which had been so exultingly attributed to a province of Mexico, colonized under her laws, was necessarily annexed to that commonwealth of Virginia, which was the first free State of this New World. Indeed, it will be always difficult to explain why Texas herself did not have at least as much legal right to go as to come.

But for JOHNSTON, as for destiny, there was but

one tribunal to which the issue was referred, and that was visibly confronting him. It was for the sword to write the record. The gage of battle was thrown down, and by JOHNSTON lifted with a knight's good conscience. What followed is written in letters of flame, and in this crude summary is only referred to as illustrative of character. For the first word and act of JOHNSTON when he drew his sword, on the side he so unreservedly espoused, prefigures his quality—the judgment as unswerving as it was intrepid, the faculty to be bold or cautious as the emergency demanded. His sure eye quickly saw that the triangle, formed by the Potomac. the Shennandoah, and Furnace Ridge, was untenable by any force not strong enough to hold Maryland Heights, which swept every part of it by enfilade and reverse fires; and that, moreover, it was twenty miles out of position to defend against Patterson's expected advance, or to prevent McClellan's junction with him. His soldierly sense informed him that Winchester was the strategic point for every purpose. There the practicable roads from west and northwest, as well as from Manassas, meet the route from Pennsylvania and Maryland. Thither, on the 15th of June, he moved his meagre force from the funnel of Harper's Ferry. On the next day Patterson crossed the Potomac. The skill with which, one month later, he eluded Patterson's army of more than thirty thousand, and hurled his own from the mountains upon McDowell, was the master-stroke of Manassas—JOHNSTON's rear column, under Kirby Smith, coming upon the field, just as Barnard Bee was falling, and Jackson's Stonewall the last Gibraltar· Just when the South Carolina Brigade was hardest pressed, an aide or courier of Bee, meeting JOHNSTON, asked, "Where are your Virginians?" "In the thickest of the fight," was the Spartan an· swer. It was a victory⁻ won by an army which it- self barely grazed defeat, and one, therefore, difficult to pursue. But in this cursory glance one thing cannot be omitted—the full credit which JOHNSTON everywhere gives Beauregard.

The bold design submitted by the military offi- cers, in a council of war, at Manassas in September, 1861, to concentrate at that point the strength of the Confederacy, even at the cost of leaving bare of de- fense points more remote, so that there might be taken an aggressive which would be decisive, is a matter of history. It is expressive of a brave but well balanced judgment, heedful and comprehensive, which sought to exchange risk where victory was not vital for where it was. It is true weighty reasons were given for overruling it. An army of sixty thous- and soldiers was the force deemed essential to such a movement. Troops to increase the army to this num- ber could only be furnished by taking them from other positions then threatened. This seemed to the Execu- tive unreasonable. New troops could not be fur- nished because there were no arms save those which were borne by the troops then in the field. Arms were expected from abroad, but had not come, and the manufacture was still undeveloped. By this council of war, a light is thrown on the military conditions, which, for succeeding months, were de- fensive only. In the penury of men and arms thereby revealed excessive forwardness was not obligatory.

But the defensive was one which, whenever as saulted, as at Leesburg, displayed an undismayed and impenetrable front.

At the close of the winter and opening of the spring of 1861, the time had come for JOHNSTON to embrace in his vision and preparation, the four routes whereby McClellan might advance—the one chosen the previous July; another by Fredericksburg; the third and fourth by the lower Rappahannock, or the Peninsula between the York and James. The choice of the second route (joined to movements which, by the aid of the river, it was easy to conceal), would place McClellan at least two days nearer Richmond than was JOHNSTON at Bull Run. Face to face with these conditions, the Confederate General, between the 5th and the 11th of March, placed his entire army on the south bank of the Rappahannock, where with equal readiness he could resist his antagonist advancing from Manassas, or meet him at Fredericksburg, and at the same time be in a position to unite with others, should he move from Fortress Monroe, or by the lower Rappahannock. On the latter date McClellan occupied the works at Centreville and Manassas, which, except by Quaker guns, had been deserted since the evening of the 9th. Fortress Monroe was then chosen as the base of operations against Richmond. Soon perceiving the evidence of this, JOHNSTON moved to the south of the Rapidan, whence he could still more effectually unite the forces of opposition to the meditated movement. McClellan's plan was to capture the force on the Peninsula, open the James and press on to Richmond before reinforcements could arrive. Two things baffled his purpose—first, Magruder's inflexible intrenchments; second, JOHNSTON'S alertness. On the day McClellan began his movement from Fortress Monroe. JOHNSTON began the movement to swell Magruder's handful. It was on the fifth of April that McClellan was brought to a halt, in front of Yorktown and the supporting fortifications. As the conclusion from the artillery duel of this day, which was protracted until dusk, it was deemed inexpedient to carry these positions by assault. It was an army of a hundred thousand against twelve. With such forces against such forts, it had been ascertained, that the ground, in front of those frowning heights and forbidding swamps, was swept by guns, which could not be silenced. Accordingly, parallels were started to bring Yorktown to terms by a more gradual procedure. There is, however, no parallel to the confession extorted from McClellan by Magruder.

From the final parallel, it was thought siege batteries would be ready to open on the 6th of May. JOHNSTON'S computation, coinciding with McClellan's, Yorktown was evacuated on the night of the 3d. On the morning of the 4th, empty works again capitulated to the conqueror.

It was at the junction of the Yorktown and Hampton Roads, at about half-past five on the morning of the 5th, that Hooker's sharp shooters, leading the pursuit, drove in the Confederate picket. It was in front of Fort Magruder, one of a cordon of redoubts, thirteen in number, which Magruder's forethought had constructed. It was just two miles from the venerable shades and spires of Williamsburg. With-

in two miles of Hooker, at the time, were thirty
thousand troops; within twelve miles the bulk of the
Army of the Potomac. He, therefore, made his dispositions to attack, so that if he did not capture the
army before him, he would at least hold it until
others could. Williamsburg was a well fought field,
where Hancock leaped to fame, and where none can
be reproached with want of valor. But the army in
front of Hooker was neither captured nor held. The
well calculated blow of Johnston was fierce and stun-
ning, and his very deliberate retreat was no more
interrupted. What most interests us to-night is the
magnanimous grace with which JOHNSTON refers to the
officer in command of the troops engaged. "About
three o'clock," he says, "I rode upon the field, but
found myself compelled to be a mere spectator, for
General Longstreet's clear head and brave heart left
me no apology for interference."

Meantime McClellan was bending every energy to
the active shipment of troops, by water, to the west
bank of the Pamunky, opposite West Point. In vain
did he seek there the unguarded spot. Just how to
strike when blows were exigent, and how to hold up
his buckler against surprise; in one instant to be
shield and spear, was JOHNSTON's secret. He had retired before overwhelming numbers with the step
and gesture of a master.

It was JOHNSTON's theory of war, that the time
for blows to be efficient was not when his enemy was
near his base, and he distant from his own; but under
exactly reverse conditions. As early as April 15th.
JOHNSTON proposed that McClellan's army should be
attacked in front of Richmond by one as numerous,

formed by uniting all the available forces of the Confederacy in North Carolina, South Carolina, and Georgia, with those at Norfolk, on the Peninsula, and then near Richmond. Such an army surprising McClellan by an attack, when he was looking to the siege of Richmond, might be expected to defeat him; and defeat, a hundred miles from his then base of supplies, would mean destruction. On the 22d and 27th he reiterates this view. A month later, the new vigor of twenty-five thousand soldiers, drawn from North Carolina and the south, added to the "red right arm" of Jackson, and launched by the genius of Lee, was the thunderbolt to rive asunder McClellan's oak. JOHNSTON's plan would have forestalled preparation by the unexpected, before a change of base was feasible.

Reasons having been presented in opposition to his original plan, Johnston's next design was to encourage an increasing interval between McClellan's troops, as the latter approached the Chickahominy, and, when he was fairly astride the little river, to attack him. He must do this before McDowell, moving southward from Fredericksburg, could swell the tide of battle against Richmond. On the morning of May 30th, reconnoissances showed that one entire corps, and a part, if not the whole of another, were on the south side of the river. In point of fact, the corps of Heintzelman and Keyes were across—the latter in advance. Heintzelman was at White Oak and Bottom's bridges, with the nearest support to him some six miles distant, on the opposite side of the stream. The Chickahominy ran between the two wings of the army. JOHNSTON now saw his opportunity, and to see it was to seize it. A violent rain storm, which fell soon after, swelling the stream, and perhaps making it impassable, convinced him that the hoped for hour had struck. His orders were at once given. Written orders were dispatched to Hill, Huger, and G. W. Smith, and in writing acknowledged. Longstreet being near headquarters received his orders verbally. G. W. Smith was to take position on the left, to support the attack which the other divisions were to make upon the right. All were to move at daybreak.

Seven Pines, which was to be the chief scene of encounter, is at the junction of the Nine Mile and Williamsburg roads. Casey's redoubt was a half mile nearer to Richmond. His division and artillery formed the first line to be attacked, the left resting upon White Oak Swamp, the right extending across the York River Railroad. White Oak Swamp, the Williamsburg road, and the railroad are nearly parallel. JOHNSTON expected the blow by his own right to be delivered before 8 A. M., and was confident, that the effect of it would be a complete victory, on the south side of the swollen Chickahominy. This opinion is fully shared by General Keyes, and published by him in his "Fifty Years' Observations."

Wherever the responsibility may be lodged for the failure to attack, not only at 8 A. M., but even as early as noon, the defect was not in JOHNSTON's orders and timely preparations. For some reason never sufficiently explained, and still matter of controversy, the attack on the right did not begin until 2 o'clock in the afternoon. But even after the delay of all these hours, the rush of

Hill and Longstreet had stormed and carried the
entrenchments opposed to them, with the camp
equipments, ordnance and stores belonging to the
troops assailed, driving Casey in utter route back
upon Conch, and Couch upon Heintzleman, when
their onward movement was stopped by the falling night. JOHNSTON had stationed himself on the
left to take part in the co-operating movement,—
where the force in front of Smith had been rescued
from defeat by Sumner's opportune arrival—and
had just ordered each regiment to sleep where it
fought, to be ready to renew the battle at dawn,
when he received a musket shot in the shoulder.
and a moment after was unhorsed by a fragment of
shell which struck him in the breast. The reins of
his steed and of his victory fell from his hands. The
brightness of his sword shone for an instant, and
then the darkness swallowed it. The sharpness of
it slept when the night became its sheath. A hero
was borne upon his shield fallen but undismayed.
Beneath the smitten breast there lived a heart un-
smitten.

When JOHNSTON was stricken down at Seven Pines.
he left an army, which had been animated by him
to a new consciousness of valor; the Army of Virginia, whose organization was the work of his hand.
Doubtless, one object of the blow was accomplished.
in the check to McClellan's advance on the south
side of the swamp. Nevertheless, as the strategy in
the valley and the leap to Manassas was the shining
image of the boldness and caution so happily mixed
in him; so Seven Pines might be construed to be the
malignant prophecy of that dark fate, which seemed

thereafter to rise in mutiny against him, and be the
incessant wound of victory. Rarely has the countenance of fate worn a look and spoken from a lip so
cynical, as in that chapter, wherein as it were, war's
master was made his victim, his own edge turned
against him. It was the superlative satire of events.
JOHNSTON's eminence was tried in the most fiery
furnace in which such energies could be constrained
to walk. The field of victory spread before him to
be organized was, with recurring bitterness, snatched
from him on the day the prizes were bestowed. We
feel as if we were witnessing less the encounter of
man with human circumstance, than the supernatural
warfare of a Titan whose fight is with the skies.

JOHNSTON reported for duty on the 12th of Novem-
ber, and on the 24th, received orders of that date,
assigning him to the command of the Department of
the West; a geographical department, including the
States of Tennessee, Mississippi, Alabama, and parts
of Louisiana, Georgia and North Carolina. Had the
reality of this command been delivered to JOHNSTON,
it would have been the very arena for the employment
of his large gifts. The vision which is competent to
survey and manage the whole landscape of war, and
direct the grand movements and general arrange-
ments of campaigns is known as strategy. Of this
great faculty JOHNSTON was the master.

The world's mad game is not played blind fold.
The genius of war, like other genius, is not the mere
gift of luck, but the consummation of a profound
attention to details and all the forces of supremacy.
The game, in which the greatest intellects are matched for the greatest stakes, must be an intellectual

game. The successful general, who succeeds against
disproportionate numbers and resources, is not a military gambler, but the closest of all close calculators.
His greatness is that when he does stand upon reality he knows it, and is not to be terrified out of it
or the daring which it justifies. This is the applica-
tion of the great saying of the Roman orator, "A
man of courage is also full of faith." Genius has
its own way of dealing with the impossible, but it is
not a senseless way, nor ever really reckless.

JOHNSTON went to the West, not to do brilliant
things for their own sake, but to win the cause of
which he was the soldier. Accustomed as he ever
was to ride in the van of danger, his bruises of battle shining like stars upon him, he was the man of
all others to be heeded, when he counselled caution.
His whole life was that glorious thing—fair combat
through strife to victory. With an unshrinking
devotion equal to any task, he proposed to his own
courageous intellect that system of the offensive-de-
fensive, which once before in the world's annals was
the salvation, and the sole salvation, of the bravest
and most determined people on its face. The greatest of all warlike races rescued itself from destruction, and the world's future empire from a rival, by
slowly learning that victories may be won by avoid-
ing no less than by seeking battle; that a march or
manoeuvre at the right time, is more potent than a
battle at the wrong time; that to seize a position
which will threaten the adverse army the instant it
does move, may far exceed the value of an attack
upon it, if it does not; that the circuit of a large and
politic strategy is wider and higher, and makes its

demands upon an intellectual grasp more subtle and more vivid, than the mere rapture of pitched battle. This was the instruction of which Fabius and Marcellus were the apt pupils, and Hannibal the schoolmaster.

It is idle now to speculate as to what might have happened, had JOHNSTON been allowed to be the real main spring of movements he was so fitted to direct : if the substance of his important command had been delivered to him. Fortune opposed him with an iron heart, which no excellence could touch. He opposed fortune with an iron will, which, unconquered and undismayed, has outlived fortune's worst and triumphed over it. His strife seems to be waged less with visible, than with some inscrutable power, which baffled, but never met him in authentic shape. It is his peculiar fame, that no disappointment and no calamity has been able to deny and to dethrone his real supremacy. All noble strength partakes of the wrestler's agony. The thing which we honor is the unshrinking dedication of thews and sinews by man to his fellows, in the face of the frown of power and in the teeth of temporal scorn. That which makes the brave man, struggling in the storms of fate, a sight for gods and men, is the magnanimity to rise from strain and overthrow, with a rectitude of will untainted and unspent; the uprightness, which, bows with bended knee before God's footstool, but not with bended neck under man's yoke, nor subjugated brow under life's oppression. The struggle of fate seemed to be to write the death-warrant of all which to JOHNSTON was most precious; but the final victory was with JOHNSTON. The moral self which was his charge to keep, the post of which he was God's sentry, was never once surprised, never once surrendered. What was then his lonely outpost is to-night his citadel.

The ink was hardly dry upon the special order assigning JOHNSTON to the Department of the West, when he promptly made known the plan of campaign which commended itself to him. Inasmuch as the army of the Trans-Mississippi was relatively strong, and the army now proposed to be placed under him was relatively weak, and the latter subject to the further disadvantage of being divided by the Tennessee River, he urged that the united force of both departments be thrown at once on Grant. As the troops in Arkansas and those under Pemberton had the same great object—the defense of the Mississippi Valley—and both opposed to troops having one object—the possession of the Mississippi—the main force of the latter operating on the east side of the river; the more direct and immediate co-operation of the former was the thing advised. He significantly adds, "As our troops are now distributed, Vicksburg is in danger." He proposed, therefore, the union of the forces of Holmes and Pemberton: those of Bragg to co-operate if practicable. By the junction he could, as he believed, overwhelm Grant, then between the Tallahatchie and Holly Springs, far from his base—the place for victory.

No notice having been taken of this plan, and suggestions made by him respecting the commands of Bragg and Pemberton, as well as objections interposed by him to the diminution of the former force to augment the latter, failing also of approval,

JOHNSTON acquired the feeling that his wide com
mand was little more than nominal. To be answer
able for issues without authority to order, or potently
advise, is "a barren sceptre" which none can grasp
with use or honor. Upon the ground that armies
with different objects, like those of Mississippi and
Tennessee, were too far apart for mutual dependence,
and, therefore, could not be commanded properly by
the same general, JOHNSTON asked to have a different
command assigned him. Ultimately a special order
did so re-assign him. Intermediately he received
specific orders directing him where to go.

It was on the 22d of January, 1863, while he was
inspecting the defenses of Mobile, that he was ordered to go to the headquarters of Bragg, for the
purpose of determining whether the latter had so far
lost the confidence of his army, as to make it expe-
dient to supersede him. If such was found to be the
fact, JOHNSTON was to be his successor. It was
hardly fair, thus to make a generous mind at once com-
petitor and judge: to place him in a position, where
his merest word would exalt himself at the expense of
the party judged. JOHNSTON threw every doubt in
favor of his companion in arms, and advised against
Bragg's removal. His letter to the Confederate President upon this subject deserves to be known more
widely than it is. "I respectfully suggest," he wrote,
"that should it then appear to you necessary to remove General Bragg, none in this army or engaged in
this investigation ought to be his successor." This is
the voice of a true knight. It is the reflex of that
grace of mind which is ever the noblest ornament to
its greatness. When death has silenced him who

wrote, it speaks to the hearts which survive, like a trumpet in the stillness of the night. He had returned to Mobile when, on the 12th of February, he was ordered to assume charge of the army of middle Tennessee. At the time the general of that army was bowed and broken by the illness of his wife, supposed to be at the point of death. With a natural chivalry, Johnston postponed the communication of the order, reporting to Richmond the reasons for so doing. Once more an act of noble grace! These are the acts which write their bright light on the human sky. When the particular crisis had passed, Johnston's own debility was such that he could not assume command, and the order was indefinitely postponed. He had reported for duty all too soon, and too severely taxed the adamant which knew so little how to yield. It was not until the 12th of March that he was able to resume his duties in the field.

Johnston had inspected Vicksburg during Christmas week, and even so early had decided, as he shortly afterwards stated to General Maury, that it was a mistake to keep in an intrenched camp so large an army, whose true place was in the field; that a heavy work should be constructed to command the river just above Vicksburg, "at the turn"—with a year's supply for a good garrison of three thousand men. Until April 14th Pemberton's telegrams indicated an effort against Bragg, in whose vicinity Johnston was, and not against Vicksburg. On the 16th of April the Union fleet passed the batteries of Vicksburg. To the mind of Johnston it was clear that, when this could happen, Vicksburg ceased to be of any more importance than any other

place on the river. On the 29th of April, and 1st
of May, Pemberton announced a movement upon
Grand Gulf, with a view to Vicksburg. JOHNSTON
replied on the instant, telling Pemberton to unite
all his troops from every quarter for the repulse of
Grant, while the latter was crossing the river, and to
move at once for the purpose—adding "success will
give you back what was abandoned to win it." On the
9th of May a dispatch was received by JOHNSTON, at
Tullahoma, in Middle Tennessee, directing him to
"proceed at once to Mississippi to take chief command
of the forces there." He replied, "I shall go immediately, although unfit for field service." From
the shell which had unhorsed him at Seven Pines,
he had not yet so far rallied as to be able to ride
into the field. But the orders he forthwith gave reflect the warrior grasp which nothing could relax.
Three things were clear to JOHNSTON; first, that the
time to attack was when the enemy was divided in
the passage of the river; second, that the invading
army must be defeated in the field, and that Vicksburg must fall if besieged; third, that Vicksburg
ceased to be of exceptional importance, after the
junction of the upper and lower fleet. In coincidence
with these views, were his orders to the officer in
command at Vicksburg; to leave the intrenchments
there, and unite with himself in an attack upon the
separate detachments of the opposing force; but in
any event, to evacuate Vicksburg and its dependen-
cies, and save the army which could not escape if
Vicksburg were besieged.

When, from a failure to execute these instructions,
Sherman, on the 13th of May, was able to interpose

four divisions at Clinton, on the Southern Railroad.
JOHNSTON, then hurrying forward with his little
army, at once ordered Pemberton to come up, with
all the strength he could assemble, in Sherman's
rear, promising his own co-operation. Clinton was
seventeen miles east of Pemberton. As is well known,
and, doubtless, because of the importance ascribed
to Vicksburg, Pemberton moved south, instead of
east, with a part only of his force, and out of reach
of the little band, waiting to participate at Clinton.
He marched to the disasters of Champion Hill and
Baker's Creek. On being so informed, in terms
which admitted of no mistake, JOHNSTON ordered
the immediate evacuation of Vicksburg and Port
Hudson.

It is not desirable to discuss the considerations,
which caused a sincerely patriotic soldier to so devi-
ate from these orders, as to invert and, in effect, to an-
nul them. JOHNSTON'S orders meant to him as he
states, "the fall of Port Hudson, the surrender of the
Mississippi River, and the severance of the Confederacy." Saving that it was already severed, this was
true. If, however, instead of deviation, there had
been execution, whether or not it would have made
the difference between the disaster which was sustained by Pemberton at Baker's Creek, and victory
at Clinton, it would certainly have made the difference between an army captured in Vicksburg and an
unconquered one outside of it. The investment of
Vicksburg was completed of the 19th, and its surrender was then but a matter of time. Mr. A. H. Stephens
states, that on the 23d of June, he was informed, at
the War Department, that the surrender of Vicks-

burg was inevitable. If the besieged could not escape
the besieger at the beginning of the siege, still less at
the end ; if the force within did not possess the power
to unite with the force without before the siege began,
how much less could it expect to effect such junction
after forty days and forty nights of exhaustion were
added to it? If the stronger force within the citadel
could not cut its way out, how much less could the
weaker force without be expected to cut its way in?
At the time JOHNSTON had but two brigades. The
race of collecting troops, wherewith to relieve the besieged, was run against those who could easily out-
strip him. After five weeks of indefatigable exer-
tion, he could only say, on the 20th of June, "when
all reinforcements arrive, I shall have about 23,000."
A twice beaten army, enclosed in Vicksburg, could
not be saved by one not equal in strength to a third
of the covering force. To have attempted it, against
strong circumvallations, would have been to complete the capture of the army within, by the wanton
massacre of the army without—to fling a second
catastrophe after the first. The fate of Vicksburg
and Port Hudson was sealed, unless an army strong
enough to carry Grant's intrenchments could be
brought to the assault.

"He should have struck a blow." it is said. To
strike a blow unwisely is one of the simplest of human
actions. It is done daily with the smallest possible
profit to mankind. It will ever be a narrow cockpit
in which the tactics of Donnybrook Fair score their
success. The shout of victory or death is irrele-
vant where death alone is possible. It is not even
to court the hazard of a die to rush to sure de-

struction. Should the general then set his cause
upon the cast, and rush into the battle merely to
die there? The rush of despair proclaims as much
fear as courage. Johnston was right. The place to
defend Vicksburg was in the field. As a beleaguered
city its defense was hopeless. Isolation was destruction. Vicksburg ceased to be of value, when its bluffs
could no longer close navigation to a hostile force,
nor keep it open to a friendly one. The army within
was invaluable, and could not be replaced. To im-
mure was to sacrifice. To shut in strength was to
shut out strength. In the great game of danger, he
wins the day who really risks the least, however he
may seem to hazard all. Courage and skill are shown
in disregarding the imminent appearance, in the confidence of victory seen through the deadly imminence.
But when to the unblenching eye of war's leader the
peril is the only reality, and the victory beyond is
the illusion, it is fatuity to strike. The perilous
movement is victorious only when it places an adversary at a real disadvantage. Instead of a concen-
tration of the weaker army, as ordered by Johnston,
so as to be able to fall upon the stronger one in detail; by the deviations from his orders, the weaker
army was so distributed as to be taken in detail by
the concentrated stronger one.

There are times in life's experience, when the winds
of fortune seem to sport with human actions; when
those we would unite with frustrate us, to their own
cost, and by their sacrifice; times when it would
look, as if some sardonic deity had been unbound to
baffle calculation; to poison the springs of action;
to shake from their centre faith and duty: to per-

plex reason and conscience : and to the death-call of a true endeavor be the mocking Mephistopheles.

Something akin to this must have been present to JOHNSTON, when he saw the strength of the West hewed in two, by movements which seemed to solicit the fortified line of the enemy to enter, like a wedge of steel, between Vicksburg and his own exterior force; when he saw the relatively strong force retire behind works because of inability to meet the enemy in the open field, and then from their walls call upon the relatively weak force to storm that same enemy in his fortifications. In such catastrophe, all that man can do is to oppose duty to dejection; make clear the record of responsibility, and follow with unfaltering step the light left in the sky. This done, the result is with the great Captain of events, who makes and unmakes life and its aims. It was the destiny of JOHNSTON to be the unhearkened Cassandra of his time, the sageness of whose counsel history will measure, by the fatality of not receiving it.

It is marvelous, that after such a calamity as that at Vicksburg, the small army which had been gathered by JOHNSTON, was pursued by no worse disaster. While Vicksburg and Port Hudson stood, and there was hope that either might be succored, Jackson was essential to the manœuvering army—the key to the position. When they fell, the military value of Jackson ended. Nevertheless, JOHNSTON drew up in front of it, inviting an assault, and only when his adversary showed he again intended to resort to the sure course of investment, did he withdraw. I believe there is no dispute that JOHNSTON's management here was one of signal ability. One of his officers, who in the later history of the war took sides with Hood, in speaking of JOHNSTON'S masterly management, at this point, added this commentary—"I may say, I never saw JOHNSTON do anything which did not seem to me better done than anyone else could do it. My only criticism is that there was not more of it." The faculty to do whatever is done better than anyone else can do it is one which is never redundant, and, therefore, one which a community struggling, in the death grips, for existence, can ill-afford to part with, and invite, to do nothing.

During the remainder of the year the operations of the Union army in Mississippi were limited to predatory expeditions. Nothing was captured which was in JOHNSTON'S custody; nothing defeated which he led.

During this summer JOHNSTON received a letter from the Confederate President, criticising his conduct and conclusions, in terms, which were hardly those to win a hero's assent. To this JOHNSTON replied with that invincible clearness of which, as of the art of war, he was the master. There would seem to be ground for the dilemma, afterwards interposed by JOHNSTON, that, if the criticisms of him were deserved, the further retention of him in command was indefensible. And his services were to be retained! Unhappily thereafter upon terms of mutual distrust between him and the authority to which he reported.

It was on the 18th of December, 1863, that JOHN-STON was ordered to assume command of the Army of Tennessee. The instructions which awaited him at Dalton advised him, that he would probably find the army there disheartened by late events, and deprived of ordnance and materials; that it was hoped his presence would do much to re-establish hope, restore discipline, and inspire confidence.

JOHNSTON succeeded to Bragg upon an unenviable throne. Whether justly or unjustly, the experiences of the preceding year had alienated the allegiance without which it was incoherent and discredited. The battle of Missionary Ridge was the greatest disaster sustained by the Confederate arms in pitched battle during the whole war. Nearly one-half the guns, caissons and munitions of the defeated army had been abandoned. Dalton had not been selected because of its defensive strength, but simply because the retreat from Missionary Ridge had ceased at that point. JOHNSTON was sent to repair disaster. The army he now commanded was the same which, under Bragg, had been routed at Missionary Ridge. Sherman's army was the one which had routed it. The defeated army had been depleted since the battle. The successful one had been augmented. JOHNSTON so reorganized and reassured his dispirited force, that, when the campaign opened in the spring, the poorest regiment he had was superior in effectiveness and drill to the best when he took command. The change was swift and permanent. Thenceforth, no army in the Confederacy excelled, if any equaled it, in drill and discipline. The whole army felt that a lofty gentleman was in command, animated by a noble and pervading justice, which no favor could bias and no incompetence mislead. The genius for rapid organization could not be more splendidly evinced. Wherever his hand was laid, a life of discipline sprang up. It was the same organizing skill which had laid the foundation of the army of the East. It was a wonderful personal influence and mastery, which thus drew to him an army acquainted chiefly with disaster. If nothing else existed to reflect his excellence, the miracle which he wrought in this transformation, from complete rout to complete confidence, from fatal chaos and dismemberment in to compact order, would, of itself, preserve for us the image of great mind's authority and magnetism. As JOHNSTON looked upon this work of his creative week, he saw that it was good.

When on the 6th of May, 1864, the duel between the two armies began, two things must be borne in mind: first, that on the preceding fourth of July, one-third of the strength of the Confederacy had fallen, in the east and in the west, at Gettysburg and Vicksburg; second, that when the policy of wearing out by attrition was inauguarated, it was desirable for the weaker party to be economical of wear and tear. The time had surely come when the Confederacy could not be prodigal of life; when it should take no step which was not calculated with disciplined precaution. It must make no mistake. The man for this supreme emergency was then at Dalton — a man with that great attribute of a leader in convulsion, the capacity to see things as they are. As with a merchant, so with a general, his first business is to know when to spend and when to spare. JOHNSTON took into consideration the natural features of the country in front; the susceptibility for defense, natural and artificial; the importance of time without disaster to his own side; the slight result of inconclusive defeat to his opponent. Only brilliant success could now be compensation for serious loss. All these were realties which he was not permitted to forget. He was now where previous adversity might be the background for the revelation of his skill— if only he was trusted! Even the Divine Hero did not do his mighty work where faith was wanting.

The chief criticism of JOHNSTON's conduct of this campaign rests on his failure to attack Sherman at Rocky Face, three miles north of Dalton, when McPherson was detached to intercept JOHNSTON's communications, by the movement through Snake Creek Gap. I believe no intelligent criticism imputes blame to him for a failure to attack at any other point. The disposition of the Confederate army about Dalton had been made in the hope that Sherman would attack with his whole force. Therefore, JOHNSTON's entire strength was concentrated there. For the moment his communications were unprotected. A mountain divided the opposing forces. The difficulty of the passes was as great to one side as the other. In these conditions to change from the defensive and yield the advantages of ground was a certain risk. On May 1st, the effective strength of JOHNSTON's army, infantry, artillery, and cavalry was 42,856. On April 10th, 1864, Sherman reported *as present for duty* 180,000 men. Out of this force he proposed to form a compact army of exactly 100,000 men, for the purpose of his

advance. The number above given is to be distin-
guished from the number borne on his rolls, which
amounted to upwards of 340,000 men. Supposing
the utmost, a victory by JOHNSTON over the 100,000
picked men, Sherman had behind him the fortified
gap at Ringgold, and behind that the fortress of
Chattanooga. Nevertheless, a division of his adversary's force—that moment of division, which is always the moment of weakness—was just the moment
which JOHNSTON was wont to seize, and he was about
to seize this, when his reconnoissances assured him
that it was the bulk of Sherman's army, which, covered from exposure by the curtain of Rocky Face,
was marching towards Resaca by Snake Creek Gap,
and could, without serious resistance, cut his con-
nections while he was engaged by the force in front.
It was the infirmity of JOHNSTON that he would not
incur great risk without reconnoissance. He would
not leap in the dark. He had the gift, as it proved
to him, the fatal gift, of always knowing what he
was about. Unless he at once intercepted Sherman
the ruin to him was certain. Months afterwards one
of his officers ventured to ask why he did not attack
at Rocky Face. The sententious reply was, "Napo-
leon once said, the General who suffers his communications to be cut deserves to be shot."

He should have fought, his critics say, "as Lee
and Jackson fought at Chancellorsville; he should
have thrown everything on the hazard of a die; complete victory in front would have been followed by
the rout of the force in the rear." Such critics
forget that the victorious army at Chancellorsville
was not one which, after complete defeat at Fred-

ericksburg, had been delivered to a new commander,
with a friendly caution, as to the probable effect of
such late tragedy upon spirit and organization.
Chancellorsville had been prepared by all the host
of victories which fought for it like another army.
That army was one which believed defeat to be impossible. The army at Dalton had never known what
real victory meant. It was of incalculable importance, that the engagement of the latter army, under
their new leader, should be sharply discriminated
from all which had preceded it. In mere bravery the
past could not be exceeded. It was the wise discern-
ing stroke of the new regime which it was essential
to infallibly impart.

Under any military conditions, one might ask, is
it wholly reasonable to exact, as a matter of strict
military right, that a general, on taking command
of an army, shall at once, without more words, be-
come a Robert E. Lee, or Stonewall Jackson, at the
highest pinacle of their earthly achievement? One
might conclude, from the inclination expressed by
some, to inaugurate the triumphs of Lee and Jackson,
at the portal of the Georgia campaign, that such in-
auguration was a matter of election and pure prefer-
ence by ambitious minds: that one, whose heart was
in the right place, might make a habit of the miltary
marvel of the war. Alas! the rarest and most for-
tunate displays of greatness, Chancellorsvilles and
Centrevilles are not creatures of suffrage; and all
who go forward on such disastrous hypothesis, in
Georgia campaigns and elsewhere, are destined to
discover, that desire, aspiration even, is not synony-
mous with faculty.

It was in this same month, after the terrible repulse of Spottsylvania Court House, that Grant made a flank movement to the North Anna, not unlike that of Sherman to Resaca. The object of Grant was by a detour eastward, around the point where the Richmond and Fredericksburg Railroad crosses the North Anna, to cut Lee's communications. Did Lee strike the force left behind? No ; nor did he attempt to strike the force sent forward before reinforcements could arrive ; but, by the most expeditious interior line, he moved his own army to Hanover Junction, where Hancock met it. Here the two parts of the Army of the Potomac were not only separated, but a river so ran between them that, to get from one of Grant's wings to the other, that river would have to be crossed twice. On the other hand, Lee had concentrated his army between the Little river and the North Anna, not only in a strong position, but so situated that it could easily act in unity, and concentrate upon either of the opposing wings. Some say Lee should have left a small part of his force to hold the intrenchments of his left, and attacked Hancock with the rest of his army.

Hancock's force did not exceed 24,000 infantry. Leaving 7,000 to hold the west face of his intrenchments, and the apex on the river, Lee might have attacked Hancock with possibly 36,000 infantry. But, as an able officer suggests, * Hancock was intrenched, and Lee well knew the advantage that gave, and that he could not afford to suffer the inevitable loss. Those who would make the Atlanta campaign exactly like Chancellorsville should remem-

*Gen. A. A. Humphreys.

ber that, from the last day's fight at the Wilderness to Appomattox, Lee attacked no more; that from this time on Lee fought only behind intrenchments: that what could be done by in 1863, could not necessarily be done in 1864.

The whole criticism of JOHNSTON strangely forgets, that the victorious results at Second Manassas and Chancellorsville were the consequences of Jackson's spring upon the rear of Pope and Hooker: and not because Jackson suffered himself to be in their predicament. The question presented to JOHNSTON at Rocky Face was, not whether he would do like Stonewall Jackson, but whether he would deliberately do like the generals whom Stonewall Jackson defeated.

Every man in authority is the shepherd of a trust; but what so sacred as the general's — lives that will step to death at his bidding. Of all fiduciaries none has such account to render as he who is commissioned to wage the fight of a people. Human life is the talent laid in his hand, to be poured out like water, if unto him it seemeth good. Of all trusts and talents this is the one to be wisely used, and in no wise abused. The policy of JOHNSTON was not the step forward which would slide three steps back, but the step back which would find the strength to stride trebly forward. It was the drawing back of the ram's foot to strike with the horns.

The movement from Dalton began on the 12th of May. Polk's advance under Loring, and Polk himself, reached Resaca from Demopolis, Alabama, on the same day. French's division of the same army joined near Kingston several days later, and Quarles'

brigade at New Hope Church on the 26th. One may
be permitted to believe that JOHNSTON incurred as
large risk, as could be exacted of a soldier and a
patriot. when he left the whole protection of his
rear to the expected arrival of this much hurried
reinforcement. The position taken at Resaca to
meet the movement through Snake Creek Gap was
made untenable, in consequence of a similar movement by Sherman towards Calhoun—the last movement being covered by a river, as the former was by
a mountain. But the ground in the neighborhood
of Cassville seemed to JOHNSTON favorable for attack, and as there were two roads leading southward
to it, the probability was that Sherman would divide
—a column following each road—and give JOHNSTON
his opportunity to defeat one column before it could receive aid from the other. He gave his orders accordingly for battle on the 19th of May. The order an-
nouncing that battle was about to be delivered had
been read to each regiment and received with exulta-
tion. The Roman signal—the general's purple man-
tle lifted in front of the general's tent—may be said
to have been given. But General Hood, owing to
information received from one of his staff, deemed
himself justified in not executing the order to himself; and the intended attack was for this cause.
abandoned. General W. W. Mackall was sent to
Hood to ask why he did not attack as ordered.
Hood sent word in reply, that the enemy was then
advancing upon him by two roads, and he could
only defend. JOHNSTON then drew up his army, on
a ridge immediately south of Cassville, to receive
the attack of the now united columns; but the

conviction of both Polk and Hood of their inability
to hold their positions against attack caused JOHN-
STON to yield his own.   He did this upon the ground
that he could not make the fight, when two of the
three corps commanders of his army were opposed to it.
Hood said that, in the position in which he then was,
he was willing to attack, but not willing to defend.
JOHNSTON's view was, that the time to attack was
when his enemy was divided, and the time to draw
together and defend was when his enemy was united.
But unless we are to reason, that when JOHNSTON
was unwilling to fight, and some of his generals willing, JOHNSTON must be wrong ; and when JOHNSTON
was willing to fight, and his generals unwilling, the
latter must be right ; it is hard to see why he should
be blamed for Rocky Face, and they uncriticised for
Cassville.   Assuredly in both instances the hesita-
tion was the honest doubt of courageous men.
Again, at New Hope Church, after Sherman's determined but vain assault, JOHNSTON made his own dispositions to attack.   Hood was to assail Sherman's
left, at dawn, on the 29th of May, and Polk and
Hardee to join in the battle successively.   At 10 A M.
Hood reported that he found the enemy entrenched
and deemed it inexpedient to attack, without fresh instructions.   The opportunity had passed.   The prop-
osition had originally come from Hood, and received
the sanction of JOHNSTON.   Hood says the opportunity had passed, not because his views had changed,
but because the situation of the enemy had changed.
Doubtless this was so.   And might not the com-
mander-in-chief of that army be permitted to assign
the identical reason for his own change of plan at
Rocky Face ?

At New Hope Church, at Kennesaw Mountain, all
that fierce attack could do was tried and found wanting. As the attack was resolute, so the repulse was
bitter. If there was no such repulse, as at Fredericksburg, Spottsylvania and Cold Harbor, it must
have been owing to the fact that there was no such
attack—persistent as Sherman's undoubtedly were.
In JOHNSTON's view, between Dalton and the Chattahoochie, the 19th and 29th of May, offered the only
opportunities to give battle, without attacking the
preponderant force in entrenchments. But Cassville
he considered his greatest opportunity.

From Resaca to Atlanta might be called a siege in
open field—daily approaches and resistances, daily
battle, so received, as to make the losses to the assailant more than treble those of the defensive forces.
Sherman's progress was at the aate of a mile and a
quarter a day. Every day was a warlike exercise.
In the warfare of attrition, at this rate of prog
ress, battle could ere long be given upon equal terms.

The advancing army found, in the wake of that retreat, no deserters, no stragglers, no muskets, no material of war. Retreat resembles victory when it is
the assailant who is chiefly worn by the advantageous
battle of each day. Think for an instant of this
single achievement, that in all the difficulty of the
time, in the imminent breach of daily battle, JOHN-
STON's troops did not miss a meal from Dalton to
Atlanta: that the primitive prayer: "Give us this
day our daily bread," was punctually answered out
of the smoke and roar of unremitting war—that too
when not only the nutrition of life but the nutrition
of death was scant; when he had to be parsimonious

of ammunition in his skirmishes, in order to be sure of it for his general engagements. He swung his army upon its hinges with the smoothness of well-oiled machinery, which no more swerved from its appointed course, than do the forces of nature, because a campaign of death reigns all around. We seem to touch the pulse of destiny itself, as we accompany that regular throb of recoil and repulse, and that still flexure of sockets about a pinion of resolve that knew no turning.

JOHNSTON felt himself daily growing stronger against an adversary daily growing weaker. Tireless in his vigilant activity, clear in his purpose, every tactical, every strategic advantage was hourly on his side. No jeopardy stole upon him unawares. With a deadly precision, he divined and repelled every adverse stroke. He handled his army as a man would the fingers of his own hand. As link by link he unwound his resource as of magic, and his determination as of steel, it was like the movement of the hand of time on the face of a clock—so imperturbable, so infallible, so inflexible, the external calm, the unhasting certainty. It was as if one fate had been found to confound another. The weak place in the joinings of his mail was nowhere found. Every blow had rebounded from him, or was parried by him. Every material preponderance had been rebuked by a general's intuition and a hero's sword. We can almost see the lion-like glare of his war-like eye, and the menacing lash of his agile movement, as rampart by rampart he retired, his relative force rising with each withdrawal, and his united living wall making his earthen wall invincible.

Missionary Ridge had made this JOHNSTON'S mission—to draw his adversary from his base and thereby compel the reduction of the force in front, by the regular growth of that required to guard the rear of each remove; to move back with such assured precaution, as never once to be surprised, nor placed at disadvantage; to skilfully dispute each foot of ground, with the least expenditure of his own forces; to thus more and more reduce the disparity existing; and warily biding his time to beckon his adversary forward, until the field of his own choice was made the final arbiter between them. And now the justifying proportions and the coigne of vantage had been won. All that executive foresight could do had been achieved. Here he would meet his foe, face to face, on ground which would equalize numerical odds. At Dalton, JOHNSTON was a hundred miles from his base. At Atlanta it was Sherman who was so separated. The fortresses which, at Dalton, Sherman had in Ringgold and Chattanooga, JOHNSTON now had in Atlanta—a place too strong to be taken by assault and too extensive to be invested. To this end Atlanta had been fortified and JOHNSTON had manoeuvred.

Now he would lay down the buckler and part the sword from its sheath. Now he would constrain fortune. Now, by his perfect sinews, he would wrest the battle wreath, which the cunning fiend had so long withheld by sinister touches on his thigh.

From Dalton to Atlanta, Sherman, by force of numbers, had been able to follow every retreat of the Confederate forces developed in their front, and then, with one or two corps, which he could afford to spare, make a flank movement imperiling their position. Three railroads then supplied Atlanta. To take Atlanta, it would be necessary to take all three. On the 17th of July, JOHNSTON had planned to attack Sherman, as the latter crossed Peach Tree Creek, expecting just such a division between his wings as Sherman actually made. He had occasion to say this, and did say it, more than once, to his Inspector General, Col. Harvie. To thus successively engage the fractions of the hostile army with the bulk of his own had been the purpose of his every movement. Success here would be decisive, he thought, by driving the defeated army against the Chattahoochie, where there were no fords, or to the east away from their communications. On the precipitous banks of the Peach Tree, the Confederate Army awaited the hour of battle. The superb strategy of their commander, and the superlative excellence of the position he had chosen, stood revealed. JOHNSTON himself, with his chief of engineers, Col. Prestman, and his chief of staff, General W. W. Mackall, was seated at a table examining the ground upon the map, and maturing the plan of battle, when the order was delivered, relieving him from command.

The goal had been reached, the victory organized; to his own vision the foe delivered into his hand, when he was again struck down; but this time, not by a blow in the breast, which at Atlanta, as at Seven Pines, was turned to the enemy. With a commanding grace in word and act, on the 17th of July he relinquished his command of the army, for which he had wrought so wisely and so well, and turned it over, with his plan of battle, to his successor, on that day appointed.

I deem it just to give verbatim the instructions of JOHNSTON to his strong, stanch hero. Gen. A. P. Stewart. "Find," said JOHNSTON to him, "the best position, on our side of Peach Tree Creek, for our army to occupy. Do not intrench. Find all the good artillery positions, and have them cleared of timber." He said that he expected Sherman would cross the Chattahoochie by the fords above the mouth of Peach Tree Creek, and advance across the creek upon Atlanta. He added that Governor Brown of Georgia had promised to furnish him fifteen thousand State militia with which to hold Atlanta, while he operated with his army in the field. He did not say that he would attack Sherman on the crossing of Peach Tree, "but," says Stewart, "his dispositions were evidently made with a view to so attack, and were inconsistent with any other purpose." That evening Stewart rode to JOHNSTON's headquarters to report that he had made the dispositions according to direction. He was met by JOHNSTON with the order for the latter's removal. Stewart has since said: "I would cheerfully have suffered the loss of either of my own arms to have been able to retain JOHNSTON in command." There could have been no purer ransom for his general's sentence than one of those stout arms. It was said by General Carter Stevenson, that he had never seen any troops in such fine discipline and condition as JOHNSTON's army on the day he was removed from command. Constancy, stanchness, erectness, governed by a true discernment, are the attributes that conquer men and events. All these attributes were with JOHNSTON's army the day he was re-

moved. Ill they recked who changed that stead-
fast camp for the meteor flash of mutability.
The authorities who made this change would rather
have been dismembered, limb from limb, than know-
ingly to have done aught injurious to their cause.
The motives for their action could be honest only,
and were urged by pressure from without, which I
doubt not was sincere. But to JOHNSTON, and as I be
lieve to history, it was as if the soldier, in his tent,
had been stabbed by his own guard.

With wounds to the body, JOHNSTON was famil-
iar; but a wounded spirit who can bear? How did
he receive this by far his severest wound? What
was the fashion of the metal which emerged from
this searching crucible? Did the equanimity which
stood by him in every other turn of fortune desert
him now? No, this did not desert him. His own
unquailing spirit was faithful to him. If in the
soldier's great campaign "no unproportioned thought
took shape in act," so now, in his unwished fur-
lough, none took shape in word. It is one of the
prerogatives of greatness to know how not to be the
sport of circumstance. Misfortune broke over him
in vain. He broke misfortune by being unbroken
by it. He was master of misfortune. The adversity,
which does not shake the mind, itself is shaken.
Nothing could be finer than JOHNSTON's demeanor
in this, his unlooked for, and, to him, unjust overthrow. Nothing froward, nothing unseemly shone
in him or fell from him. He was one whom the external universe might break, but could not bend to
an ignoble use. His tall branch stood, like the sap
of Lebanon, rooted in the real. There it stands to-

day, and will to-morrow. The forest of appearance, that has no root, falls to swift decay around it.

I bestow no particular praise on one for following conviction, albeit without the place proportioned to desert. A mercenary hero is a solecism. No one wins eminence by disregard of selfish interest in an army where it is universal. Virtue is tried by finer measures in that history. No corrupt, no venal thing survives to tarnish it. But of all adversity, there could be none more exquisitely fitted to freeze a noble heart, than that which befel the General of the West. How much easier to bear the most cruel blow of adversaries, when on either side are sustaining arms; when the strength of sympathy invests the overthrown with a dignity almost divine—the might of that incalculable arm which we call sympathy! But when, to his own view, his own stronghold is his worst hostility, when there is no supporting elbow within touch, as he looks out upon the hopes which can only ripen in his ruin, how clear in conscience, how tenancious and erect, in spiritual power and purpose, the dethroned must be to be unvanquished! The day of JOHNSTON's dethronement was his imperial day. It was the empire of a soul superior to every weapon.

The great campaign, by which he will be forever judged, is now beyond the wounds of the archers, beyond all slings and arrows, above and beyond outrageous fortune. From the dark defile of Rocky Face to the large prospect of Atlanta, it will be not only a possession, but a pattern for all time. Its rugged scenery is illuminated by the meaning with which the lines of greatness clothe the impassive and the obdurate. It has been made the mirror of a great mind. The map of it, the more it is studied the more clearly will evince, in due expression and proportion, and colors ineffaceable, the lineaments of a giant. It will be a canvas bringing to light that surpassing victory, which cancels adverse fate, and shines over it and through it.

It was upon a burning deck that JOHNSTON was next summoned to the wheel. It was night when his star again began to burn. The Confederacy was in the article of death, when it once more sent for him, whose hand nowhere appears in the drawing of that article. JOHNSTON was sent for to repair the ruin, which he at least did not prepare; to take anew the shattered remnant of that army, wrought into such firmness by him, shattered by others; but which, though shattered, was still firm to him. The Confederacy lifted up its eyes, and beheld all that was left of the Army of Tennessee, tossing and drifting like seaweed in the Carolinas, and a voice which no authority could subdue was heard crying: "All that is left to us is Thermopylæ. Oh, for a JOHNSTON to stand there!" And a firm voice answered: "I will stand in the gap." The great gap he had to fill was the one which had been rent in his devoted files by futile battle. It was Thermopylæ, not in the beginning, but at the end of warfare. With the portents of downfall all around him, his erectness was untouched ; his plume was still a banner : his name a talisman. The moral and military force, which had

been lost in JOHNSTON, will be measured for all time,
by the events of the interval, between his enforced
abdication and patriotric resumption of command.
The impending wreck of things rallied of its own
accord upon the disinherited knight. The hopes of
which his downfall had been the pedestal were now
themselves a ruin. Out of the lime pit of their destruction, out of their crash and chaos, rose from the
rejected stone the straightness of the Doric Column.

At this time it was plainly Sherman's plan to
march through the Carolinas to the rear of Lee.
When the western army went to pieces in hopeless
wreck, in front of Nashville, the one hope of the
Confederacy was the defeat of Sherman, by all the
forces which could be assembled in the Carolinas,
united to those of Lee; whenever the latter could
most effectually withdraw from the lines at Peters-
burg. Everything depended upon the success of this
movement, and the subsequent union of the same
forces against Grant. The task had sufficient elements of difficulty as originally presented. Just at
this time a new one was introduced. On the 14th
of January, Schofield had been ordered from Clifton,
on the Tennessee River, to Annapolis. From this
point he had been carried by water to North Carolina, where he united to his own army the corps of
Terry.

From the time Sherman left Atlanta every wave of
opposition had calmed in his front. He could march
to the sea or to the mountains as he pleased. The
indications were that the mighty host, which had
marched through Georgia in such comfort, would
cross the Cape Fear at Fayetteville, to be joined

there by Schofield, when, on the 22d of February, 1865 the day he was restored to command—Johnston was ordered "to concentrate all available forces and drive back Sherman." The order was one less difficult to give than to execute. It was a question on the first of March, which would reach Johnston first, his own troops from Charleston, or Sherman's army. Hardee did, indeed, cross the Pedee, at Cheraw, on the morning of the 3d, but his rear guard was so hard pressed, that it had hardly time to destroy the bridge after passing over it. On the evening of the same day, information was received that the broken columns of the Army of Tennessee had reached the railroad at Chester. Sherman's order of march encouraged the hope, that the tatters of the Confederacy might be gathered up in time to engage one of his wings. It was, however, not only Sherman, but Schofield, then marching up the Neuse from New Berne, with whom conclusions must be tried.

It was under such conditions that Johnston exposed to the world the electric force and vivid lightening of his arm. Here he gave the lofty answer, he scorned to make in words, to all who dared taunt him with want of daring. It should be some one, not less seamed over with honorable scars, who makes that charge. The battle furrowed chieftain might have said: "Put your fingers in my wounds, all ye who doubt." But the heroic answer ever is in deeds. So answered the captain, "who careless of his own blood was careful of that of his men, who knew how to take them under fire and how to bring them out."*

Report of L. P. Wigfall in the Senate of the Confederate States, March 1865.

From first manœuvre to final onset nothing can surpass the magnificent strategy he now displayed. It will have to blush before no other of the war or of the world. With decisiveness of command, which was met by celerity of execution, he at once ordered the movements which snatched, from the very jaws of death, the last Confederate victory. In the thrilling game of chess, which he now played, no pawn was taken without his leave, while he darted forward and backward upon the board, each time giving check to the king. That game was played with the coolness and consummate skill of a master hand, which knew no pause, no tremor, no uncertainty, and only lacked the force of numbers, which genius could not create, to shine by the side of Austerlitz. It was the grand audacity of a conscious master, whose nerve matched his skill; whose ministers were strength and swiftness. His first movement was with the troops of Bragg's then near Goldsboro, added to those of D. H. Hill, just arrived from Charlotte, to strike Schofield at Kinston. The blow was sufficient to scotch Schofield's advance.

Bragg's troops and those of the Army of Tennessee, were now ordered to Smithfield, midway between Raleigh and Goldsboro; it being at the moment uncertain through which of these places Sherman's route would be. Hardee was instructed to follow the road from Fayetteville to Raleigh, which, for thirty miles, is also that to Smithfield. On the 15th of March Hardee had reached Elevation on the road to Smithfield. On the 18th Hampton reported that Sherman was marching towards Goldsboro; the right wing on the direct road from Fayetteville had crossed

the Black Creek; the left on the road from Averys-
boro had not reached that stream, and was more
than a day's march from the point in its route opposite to the hamlet of Bentonville, where the two
roads according to the map of North Carolina were
twelve miles apart.

Upon this JOHNSTON prepared to attack the left column of Sherman's army before the other could support it. by ordering the troops at Smithfield and at
Elevation to march immediately to Bentonville (where
the road from Smithfield intersected that from Fayetteville to Goldsboro), to be in time to attack the next
morning. By the map. the distance from Elevation
to Bentonville was about twelve miles. In two important respects the premises of action proved incorrect.
The distance between Sherman's forces was exagger-
ated. and between his own reduced from the truth.
Thereby he was prevented from concentrating in
time to fall on one wing while in column on the
march. The sun was just rising on that beautiful
Sabbath in March, when all except Hardee had
reached the point of rendezvous. The gap made by
his absence, was for the time filled by the batteries
of Earle and Halsey.

On the way to the attack, and just in time for battle, JOHNSTON had met the shreds and patches of his
old troops, under the stanch A. P. Stewart. The best
interpreter of a General's strength is the sentiment
with which he animates his rank and file. The wild
enthusiasm of these Western troops, whenever they
caught sight of their old chief, was in itself an in-
spiration of success. It was evident that they were
as confident under him, as if they had never seen the

days which tore them into strips. They felt they had a general whose life or whose fame was as dust in the balance where his duty weighed; under whom death itself was not in vain. The force, which had been wedded to him by the campaign from Dalton to Atlanta, had not been put asunder by the Tophet of Tennessee. At last the way-worn troops under Hardee, which had marched day and night to join battle, appeared upon the scene. The use for them was quickly revealed. All told, the torn remnants made an army of less than 15,000 men. At their head, JOHNSTON burst upon Sherman's left wing, with an electrical intensity which will live in military annals as an object-lesson to show how a wasted force is endowed by a general's fire. The battle of Bentonville is that marvel—that final battle of the Confederacy which shed the last radiance on its arms as its candle flickered in the socket.

The batteries which had held the gap were now told to follow the dark plume and bright courage of Walthall, who commanded all that was left of Polk's corps. Hardee led the charge of the right wing. With an annihilating fury, the hurricane of war swept Sherman from his first and second line, and on the 19th of Marchnight fell upon JOHNSTON's victory. Had there been no other column to reckon with, or had not the discrepancy existed between the map and the facts, the blow which staggered would have prostrated. The victor would then have turned to throw his whole army upon Schofield. As it was, on the 20th, the right wing of the enemy came up. On the 21st Sherman's united army was in position on three sides of JOHNSTON. To oppose the increas-

ing coil the line of the latter was bent into a horse
shoe shape, the heel being the point of the one bridge
left, the bridge at Bentonville over Mill Creek.

The time had come for the man of resource to make
his exit. It was essential to make the road over that
bridge as secure as a turnpike in time of peace. He
knew well how to do it, not with fear but with confidence. Once more he looked to Hardee to deal
the blow he wanted. That intrepid man, first kiss-
ing the pale lips of his dying boy, borne by him on the
field, turned to the nearest cavalry command, and
assuring them he had been Captain of Dragoons
himself, and knew how to handle cavalry, ordered a
charge. On his magnificent black steed he led them,
and poured their torrent on the opposing front—
running back the skirmish line on the line of battle,
and the first line on the second. Victory made
the isthmus of contention safe. The nettle had been
rifled of its danger. Then, with forces vastly more
confident than when the fight began, JOHNSTON with-
drew with the loss of a single caisson, from between
the jaws of death, by the one opening left. Like a
whirlwind he came, and like an apparition departed.
Under arduous conditions, he had set upon a hill
that most admired faculty of man—the faculty to
seize and to use opportunity. At his side hung the
weapon—drawn from a great general's arsenal—the
energy to fuse the fickle conditions of an instant into
the bolt of victory.   •

One may be permitted to believe that, with a natural sense of vindication, he had, in this warrior
fashion, and with a warlike grace, inscribed upon

the record of the time the quality of his arm; and
with it the reasonable proof, that if the JOHNSTON
at Atlanta had not been removed, history would
have engraved for him the epitaph:

"Unus homo nobis cunctando restituit rem."

One who saw him, writes*, "As he listened to the
receding fire of the foe, the brightness of his eye
showed the satisfaction with which he looked on the
restored spirits of his old comrades in arms; and I
was touched by the affectionate manner in which he
ministered to the comfort of, and the words of cheer
which he gave to a number of wounded men who
were carried by. I could then well understand the
affection which was demonstrated by them at every
sight of him."

In 1875, Sherman wrote: "With the knowledge
now possessed of his small force, I, of course, com-
mitted an error in not overwhelming JOHNSTON'S
army on the 21st of March, 1865." It was the as-
cendancy of the few over the many. In the last
ditch JOHSTON'S victory had been won—when there
was little left beyond the field he had filled with his
valor. His cynical fate poured all its craft into this
last scoff, which left the truth illustrious when it
could no more avail a perishing cause. It was as if
his brow were torn with a mock crown at last.

Sherman now moved on to Goldsboro and effected
the junction with Schofield, which could no longer
be prevented.

JOHNSTON marched to the vicinity of Raleigh, and

* Capt. Wm. E. Earle.

disposed his troops, so that Sherman could not go forward to Virginia, without exposing his flanks; while at the same time he placed himself so as to facilitate his junction with Lee, whenever the time should come to unite once more the two, who rode into Vera Cruz together, for their last salutation of devoted valor. The respect, which these successive revelations of resource and energy excited, is, perhaps, illustrated in the terms which, on the 18th of April, Sherman accorded to JOHNSTON; and which, had they been ratified, would have saved the south the sorrow, and the North the shame—of the Reconstruction Era. The current of events chose otherwise; but once more JOHNSTON did all that sagacity could do to stem the current. To the last there was no spot upon his breastplate which his adversary's steel had pierced; none which there was undue eagerness to challenge. From crown to sole he blazed in complete proof. At the end, his line was an undefeated and unbroken line. When the Great Umpire threw down his warder, the defense of North Carolina, covered with dust and bloody sweat, was standing with firm-planted feet against assault. There it was standing when the edifice of the Confederacy fell—the last wall of its strength. It was bearing aloft its ensigns, "torn but flying," when the earth under it opened Doubtless it is the spectacle of deeds and energies like these which caused the eloquent soldier, Colonel Edginton, to declare that the force and vitality of JOHNSTON'S character was like the ocean wave—not to be measured in time of storm, nor to be fairly estimated until rivalries have ceased.

With the return of peace, JOHNSTON was removed
from the field of duty wherein he was best fitted to
win renown, and where he had woven the texture of
a character as fine as it was firm. For the most part
his fine assemblage of endowments lay like a book
within its clasp, or like a coal unkindled. Broken
by intervals of important duty, for a quarter of a
century, JOHNSTON found himself doomed to a life
of comparative inaction. There have been few to
whom it could be more trying to take off the chariot
wheels of life's activity. Perhaps one of the hardest
of the many trials of his patience was thus to loiter
by compulsion on the way where he was wont to
spur. To a breast, ever thrilling with the impulses
of action, patience was made perfect by this last
trial. Yet it were wrong to pass without a word
the blessing Heaven did not deny him; the meet
partaker of his puissance and his pang, who
drank of the same cup with him, exalting and
exalted by it; who gave him truth for truth, and,
under all the blows of time, a constancy fixed in
heaven—that blessing which, however, the world
might rock, was truer than the needle to the
pole—the blessing of a wife's true heart. And
when of this blessing, too, he was bereft, we all were
witnesses to the chastening touch of a brave man's
anguish; how sorrow falling upon a character of
such strength and depth did not harden, but melted
to a tender glory; how the snows of his last years
were irradiated by a soft, benignant light, as of sun-
set on the Alps. 'This was the final forge in which
the iron of his nature was softened to take a new
existence and more exquisite temper. He was the

picture of the veteran, sitting in the evening before his tent, all unbroken by the years which are so wont to break. He was the even more splendid picture of an elevation which was not fortuitous, nor dependent upon fortune, as he sat, still erect, amid the ruins of his heart, and the storm of life and fate.

So he lived amongst us, his upright, straightforward, unaffected life. So, as he lived and moved, the shadows of the dark reaper deepened round him, until at last we saw him standing, on the confine of of the great night. In his 85th year, there he stood, "worn, but unstooping." Nowhere could one see a countenance and frame, more worthy to declare—

"The living will that shall endure
When all that seems shall suffer shock."

One who came within the circuit of this sceptre of majestic age, might well pause to speculate whether the iron sleep could steal upon the lids, over which that iron will stood sentinel. He, too, could not be conquered until worn out by attrition. He could not be conquered then. The last foe of all he turned to meet, in the old knightly fashion, and wrung from him the final victory, wherein he who conquers self is conqueror of death. Faithful son of the church, he received his death wound, too, in the breast. Before the Universal Conqueror he fell upon his unsurrendered shield. He fell like a soldier. Closing his eyes to earth, and opening them to Heaven, he gave his soul

"Unto his Captain, Christ,
Under whose colors he had fought so long."

To this last Captain, who heareth and absolveth,

his last report is handed. "There," he said, on his death bed to Dabney Maury, "we shall surely meet." Ah, there! In the light of that perfect eye which looks clean through appearance, and judges the real only: there is his great appeal! In those upper fields, where the venom of this earth is slain, its serpent crushed; where no false balance is and no inadvertency; his clear spirit will join and be felt, where the mighty influences of time, purged of their dross, encounter, as the stars in their courses fight. On the bosom of the Infinite, he, too, is a star. In that last bosom, where the revenges of time are folded, earth's scarred warrior hath cleft a way to peace.

———o———

www.ingramcontent.com/pod-product-compliance
Lightning Source LLC
Chambersburg PA
CBHW031929060726
47496CB00008BA/2713